Dolly and Ike
CHERRY BLOSSOM TIME

written by

Richard Wallace Carr

illustrated by Mary Ashby Parrish

Dicmar Publishing

Good morning! Good morning!
Welcome to Washington DC
and the Willard Hotel.

We are your ambassadors of goodwill.
I'm Dolly and he is Ike.

This is a very special place where memories are made.

THE WILLARD

We have special rooms and special places and very special people.
And there are so many memories to share. I especially like the stories.
This is Cherry Blossom time. The hotel dresses for the occasion.
Along Peacock Alley, in the lobby…

WE'RE IN THE PINK.

Why, if it isn't my two favorite ambassadors.
Dolly and Ike. What can I do for you this beautiful morning?

Mr. Houdré is there a story in the Willard's past
that has something to do with cherry blossoms?

Come and sit down,
it just so happens that there is a very interesting story.
Do you know who was the first person from America
to make an official visit to Japan, Ike?

Why, I think it was Commodore Perry.

You are exactly right.
Our country made an official visit in 1853
and negotiated a treaty for commerce and friendship.
What do you suppose happened next?

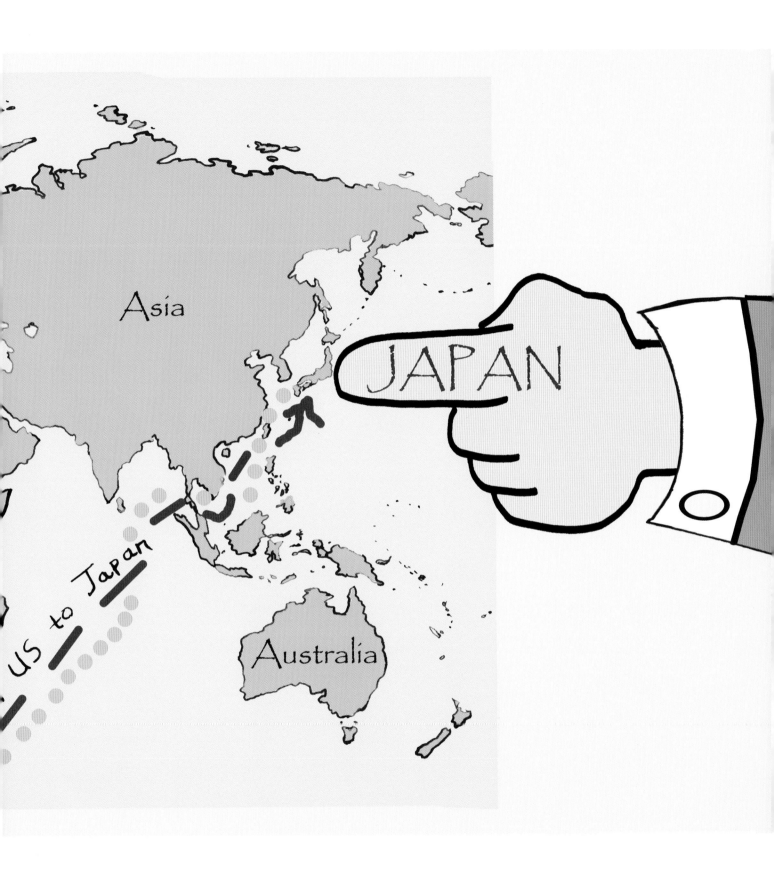

The Japanese made an official visit here?

You are so right.

This was a very special visit because no one from Japan
had ever visited America, and we had to make sure
that everything went just right.

Mr. Willard made very special arrangements.

The visitors were to have their own floor, their own kitchen and they had a separate entrance on Fourteenth Street.

When did they get here?

The Japanese arrived on May 15, 1860. There was great fanfare. Cannons were fired off and there was a parade.

Wow, look at the clothes.

And, look at the swords.

*Yes, you see the Japanese looked
and dressed very differently from us.*

These robes are beautiful.
It reminds me of kimonos, and the pants are so pretty.
I love the feel of silk.

That was the official dress of Japanese Ambassadors.

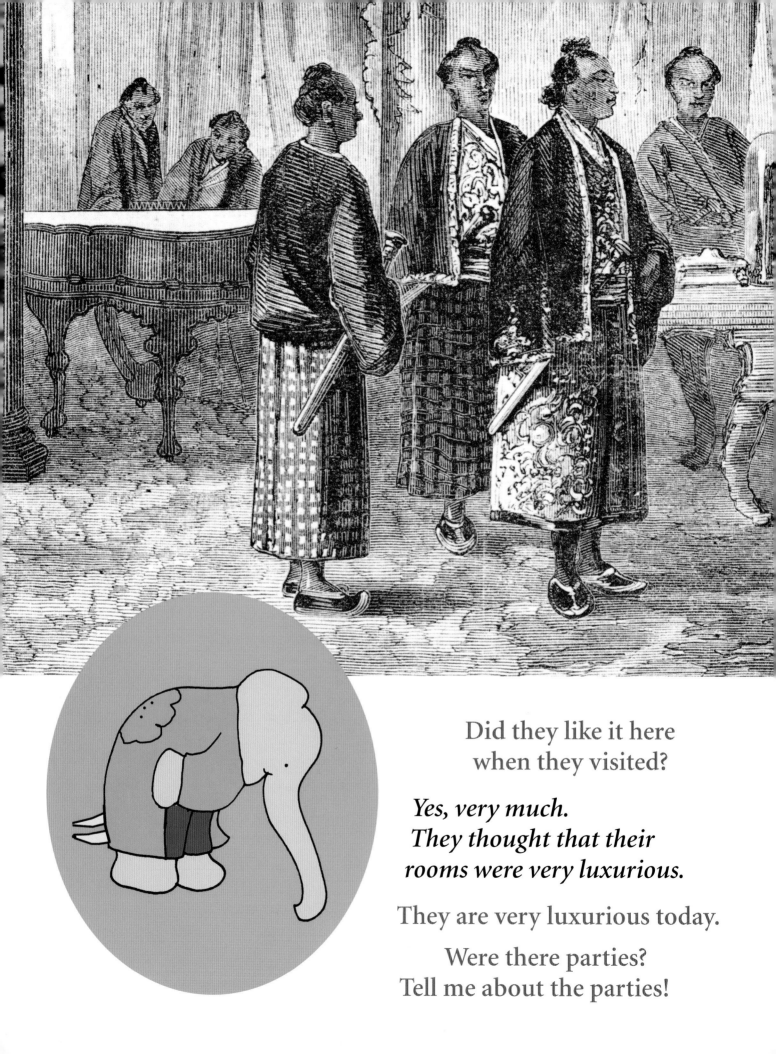

Did they like it here
when they visited?

Yes, very much.
They thought that their
rooms were very luxurious.

They are very luxurious today.

Were there parties?
Tell me about the parties!

There was much official business.
They met President Buchanan
and presented him with the treaty
which he signed for all to see.
There were balls which amused
the Japanese. They had never seen
dancing or ladies in hoop skirts.
Everyone had a lot of fun.

I wish I had a hoop dress.
I would be the belle of the ball.

Did they bring
the cherry trees?

*No, the cherry trees
actually came fifty
years later.*

*A lady named Eliza
Scidmore had seen some
beautiful cherry trees while
traveling in Japan and when
the city fathers began to beautify
the mall along the Potomac River
she recommended planting cherry trees.*

Oh, how beautiful!

So, did they plant the trees?

Actually, Eliza lobbied for 25 years.
Finally, Mrs. Taft, the President's wife, said that she liked
the idea and on March 27th, 1912 Mrs. Taft and Viscountess
Chinda, the wife of the Japanese Ambassador, planted the
first of 3,000 trees sent as a gift by the City of Tokyo.

Oh, I think I will be a Viscountess.

Did they give us any more gifts?

Yes, they have Dolly.

In 1954 to celebrate the 100th anniversary of the treaty of friendship that Commodore Perry signed, the Japanese Ambassador gave the city a 300-year-old stone lantern. Each year, the National Cherry Blossom Festival is officially opened by lighting this lantern.

And in 1958, they gave us a small stone Japanese Pagoda.

A Cherry Blossom Queen is selected and given a crown to wear.
Mikimoto Pearls donated the ceremonial crown in 1957. It has over 1,500 pearls.

Each year the Smithsonian holds a Kite Festival on the National Mall during Cherry Blossom Time.

National

Ever since that day, we have been celebrating cherry blossoms in Washington.

When was the first
Cherry Blossom Festival?

The first festival was held in 1935.

And the pageant began in 1940.
Ever since that day, we have been celebrating the National Cherry Blossom Festival.

And so the Tidal Basin has always been a calm and peaceful place with beautiful blossoms.

They make me feel like I'm in a beautiful dream.

Well, not always peaceful, Dolly.

In 1938, when they started to build the Jefferson Memorial, some ladies vowed to chain themselves to the cherry trees so they wouldn't be chopped down, and just a few years ago trees were mysteriously falling down and we found a family of beavers who needed to be moved to a new home.

Oh, I love beavers, they're so cuddly.

So, the Willard was the first to welcome a Japanese delegation to the United States.

And, Washington has become a beautiful home for
cherry trees. What a great story. I'm exhausted.

Thank you so much Mr. Houdré.
I think we'll go down to the Tidal Basin now.
We need a little peace and tranquility.

THE END.

THE HISTORY OF THE CHERRY TREES IN WASHINGTON, DC

Creation of the Tidal Basin Park

As the City of Washington and the area of the Mall grew, Congress began taking steps to ensure the creation of open spaces and the improvement of land along the Potomac River. Congress designated the area around the Tidal Basin a public park for the "scenic pleasure of the people". At that time there was also a speedway in Potomac Park. These public open spaces became the object of many plans for beautification.

Beautification and Arrival of the First Cherry Trees

In 1885, Mrs. Eliza Scidmore returned from a trip from Japan filled with excitement about the beauty of Japanese cherry trees. She made a proposal that they be planted along the Potomac waterfront to beautify the river to the government. Unfortunately, the Superintendent of Public Buildings and Grounds turned down her proposal. Mrs. Scidmore lobbied for twenty four years before she succeeded. In 1909, when she had decided to try to raise the money herself to buy cherry trees and then donate them to the city, she happened to write the President's wife, Mrs. Helen Herron Taft, to inform her of this idea. Mrs. Taft, as it happened, had also lived in Japan and was familiar with the beauty of the Japanese cherry trees. She immediately endorsed Mrs. Scidmore's idea and suggested that the trees be planted along the river by the speedway.

At the same time, a Japanese doctor visiting Washington, Dr. Jokichi Takamine, heard of the cherry tree plan and got the idea of donating more trees to beautify the city and through the Japanese counsel, Mr. Midzuno, met with Mrs. Taft who agreed to accept a gift of 2,000 trees to be given in the name of the City of Tokyo. On December 10, 1909, 2,000 cherry trees arrived in Seattle and they were shipped to Washington where they arrived on January 9th, 1910. Sadly, the Department of Agriculture found that these trees were infested with insects, and they had to be destroyed.

Second Shipment and Planting of the Cherry Trees

After everyone had expressed deep regret over the loss of the trees, Dr. Takamine agreed to donate the cost of a new shipment of trees, this time 3,020. Special precautions were taken to prepare trees that would be hardy and free of disease. In February of 1912, the new shipment of cherry trees was shipped from Yokohama to Seattle. These trees arrived in Washington on March 26th in good condition. While there were twelve different varieties, most of the trees were the popular "Yoshino" cherry tree. On March 27, 1912, First Lady Taft and Viscountess Yoshinda, the wife of the Japanese Ambassador, planted the first two cherry trees on the northern bank of the Tidal Basin. At the conclusion of the ceremony, Mrs. Taft presented the Viscountess with a bouquet of American Beauty roses. The original two trees are still standing today.

For the next seven years, workmen planted Yoshino trees around the Tidal Basin. Yoshino and other varieties were planted in East Potomac Park.

First Cherry Blossom Festival

In 1935, the first Cherry Blossom Festival was held sponsored by local civic groups, and by 1940 this had grown into a pageant. In 1948, each state selected a Cherry Blossom Princess and a queen was selected to reign during the festival. In 1952, Japan asked for our help in restoring the grove where our cherry trees came from, and the National Park Service shipped budwood from descendants of the original cherry trees back to Tokyo for restoration.

Additional Gifts from Japan to Washington DC

On March 30, 1954, Sadao Iguchi, the Japanese Ambassador to the United States, presented a 300-year-old Japanese stone lantern to the City of Washington to commemorate the 100th anniversary of the Treaty of Peace, Amity and Commerce signed by Commodore Matthew Perry in Yokohama in 1854. The lantern is 8 feet high and weighs 20 tons. Today the National Cherry Blossom Festival is started by lighting this lantern.

Since that time, several more gifts have been received from Japan. In 1957, Mr. Yositaka Mikimoto, the President of Mikimoto Pearls donated a crown used in the coronation of the Cherry Blossom Queens. The crown contains two pounds of gold and 1,589 pearls. On April 18, 1958, a Japanese pagoda carved out of stone was presented to the City of Washington to symbolize the friendship between Japan and the United States, and in 1965, the Japanese Government presented Lady Bird Johnson with 3,800 Yoshino trees for her beautification plans for the city. The First Lady and the wife of the Japanese Ambassador, Mrs. Ryuji Takeuchi, once again reenacted the planting ceremony of 1912. For the last 25 years, Washington and Japan have exchanged cuttings to preserve the lineage of the Yoshino trees for future generations.

Dedicated to:

To my wife Marie and
daughters Kate, Ann and Beth...*RWC*

To my daughters Erin and Katy...*MAP*

Illustrations by Mary Ashby Parrish

Book design by Innovative Projects, Inc.

Printed in China

ISBN: 0-933165-09-9

1 3 5 7 9 10 8 6 4 2
First Edition

 Published by Dicmar Publishing
Washington, DC
1-202-342-2231
www.dicmar.com

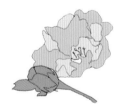